WHINY WHINY RHINO

written & illustrated by
McBoop

Blue Blanket Publishing
Auburn, Maine

For our family, friends & pachyderm pals
And especially for our favorite little whiner,
Tiny Tiny Eevee

Blue Blanket Publishing
16 Poland Spring Rd, Auburn, Maine 04210

Interior typeface is Hockey is Lif designed by Tom Murphy 7
Cover typeface is Big Top designed by Shamrock Int.

Library of Congress Control Number: 2014939502

ISBN 978-0-9903623-1-9

For more information, printables, games, merchandise
and other fun activies, please visit:

whinyrhino.com

Tiny Tiny Rhino
never seemed to have fun.
He was easily frightened
and worried a ton.

He had three big brothers who loved to play rough.
They pestered him daily to act much more tough.

His brain became filled with **WORRY** and **DREAD**

snicker snicker snicker snicker snicker snicker

As the words of his brothers
rang out in his head.

He put on a brave face as he went on his way,
and soon spotted friends who wanted to play.

Tiny Tiny Rhino, will you come kick the ball?

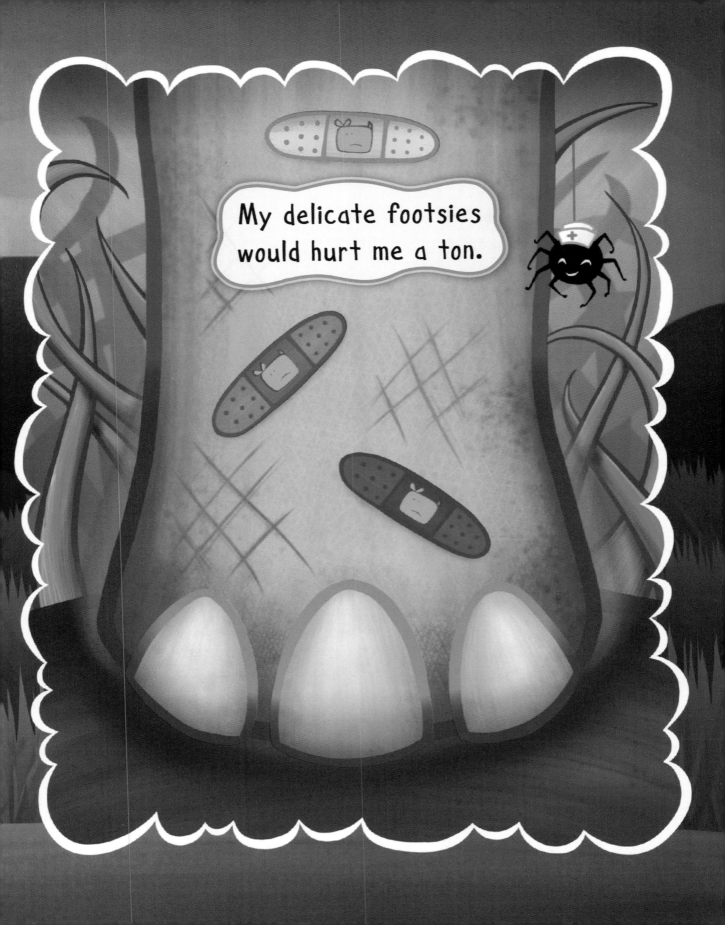

Poor Tiny said nothing.
He just ran away.

If I could do my day over, I would shine and not whine.
I'd think less of my worries, and I bet I'd be fine.

He might have had fun if he tried something new.
And suddenly, Tiny knew what to do!

He had his mind set upon making amends,
so he went back outside to find all his friends.

He spotted them headed to Crazy Croc's Drop.
They were dragging a wagon up to the top.

I'm sorry for
being so whiny all day.
I guess that my worries
got carried away.

He forgot all his fears
as they zoomed down the hill,
and soon he was cheering,
enjoying the thrill.

They crash-landed, laughing
and they could all see
that their friend, Tiny Rhino,
was purely happy.

And so Tiny realized his brothers were wrong, you don't have to be tough or particularly strong. If you want to have fun, all you must do is be willing and open to try something new.

Let's do it again!